PUF

THE BUGALUGS BUM THIEF

Tim Winton was born in Perth in 1960. Apart from some time in Europe he has always lived in West Australia. He now has two boys and a girl, a house, some chooks, ducks and a dog and lives in a tiny crayfishing town a bit like Bugalugs. He spends his time fishing, diving and surfing, and to pay for all this fun he writes books. This is his tenth.

Other books by Tim Winton

AN OPEN SWIMMER

SHALLOWS

SCISSION

THAT EYE, THE SKY

MINIMUM OF TWO

IN THE WINTER DARK

JESSE

LOCKIE LEONARD, HUMAN TORPEDO

CLOUDSTREET

BY

TIM WINTON

ILLUSTRATED BY CAROL PELHAM-THORMAN

PUFFIN BOOKS

Puffin Books
Penguin Books Australia Ltd
487 Maroondah Highway, PO Box 257
Ringwood, Victoria, 3134, Australia
Penguin Books Ltd
Harmondsworth, Middlesex, England
Viking Penguin, A Division of Penguin Books USA Inc.
375 Hudson Street, New York, New York 10014, USA
Penguin Books Canada Limited
10 Alcorn Avenue, Toronto, Ontario, Canada M4V 3B2
Penguin Books (N.Z.) Ltd
182-190 Wairau Road, Auckland 10, New Zealand

First published by Penguin Books Australia Ltd 1991

10 9 8 7 6 5

Copyright © Tim Winton, 1991
Illustrations Copyright © Carol Pelham-Thorman, 1991

All rights reserved. Without limiting the rights under copyright reserved above, no part of this publication may be reproduced, stored in or introduced into a retrieval system, or transmitted, in any form or by any means (electronic, mechanical, photocopying, recording or otherwise), without the prior written permission of both the copyright owner and the above publisher of this book.

Produced by McPhee Gribble
56 Claremont Street, South Yarra, Victoria 3141, Australia
A division of Penguin Books Australia Ltd

Typeset in Plantin by Bookset, Melbourne
Printed in Australia by The Book Printer

National Library of Australia
Cataloguing-in-Publication data:
Winton, Tim, 1960–
The Bugalugs bum thief.
ISBN 0 14 034734 8.
I. Title
A823.3

McPhee Gribble's creative writing programme is assisted by the Australia Council.

For Jesse, Harry and Alice

Skeeta Anderson woke up one summer morning to find that his bum was gone.

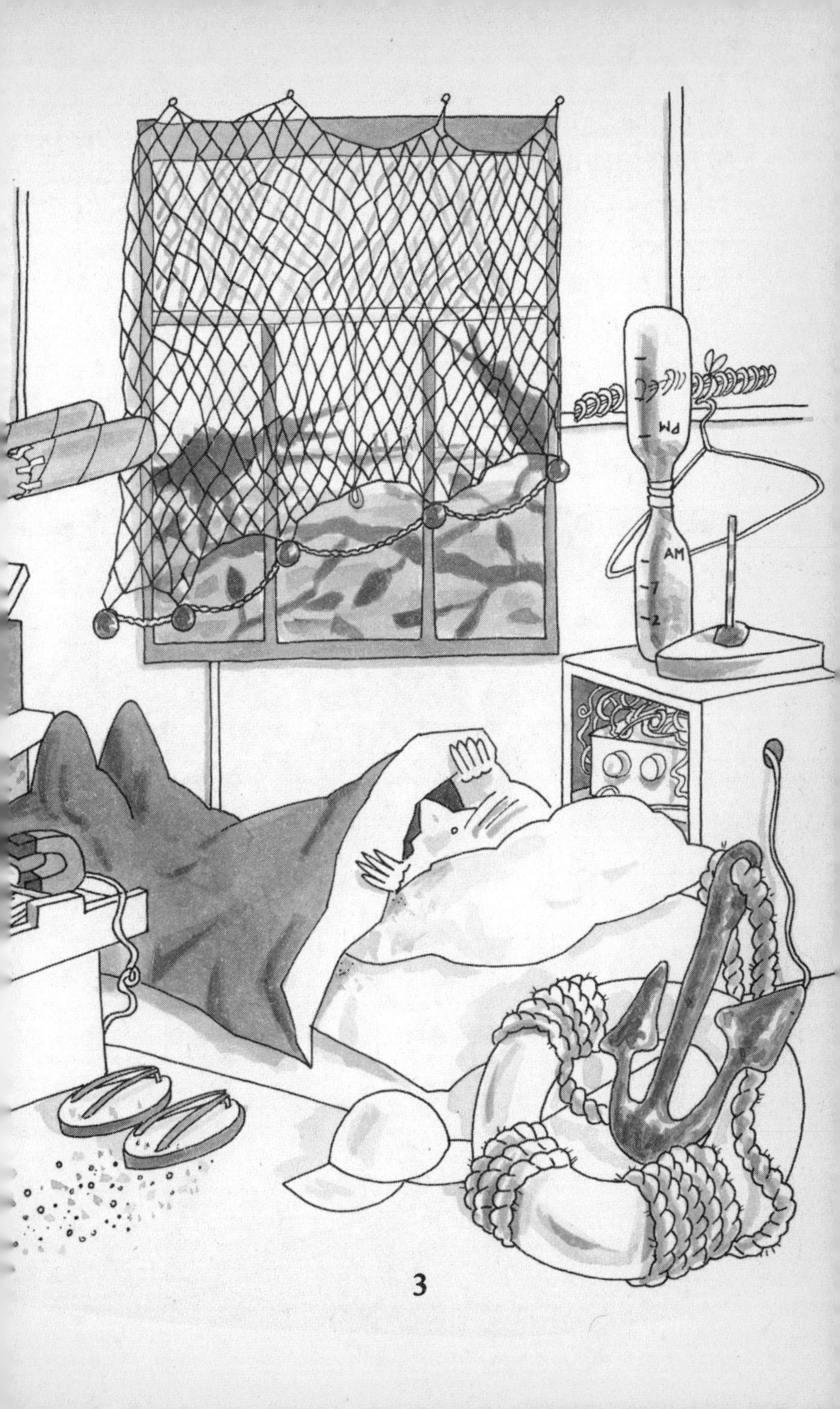
PM
AM

He lay back on his bed and tried not to get upset. I'm still asleep, he thought, I'm dreaming! But he could hear crows cawing in the tree outside his window – blaah, blaah, blaah! And he heard boat engines starting up down at the jetty, too, so he knew he was awake.
He was *not* happy.

Skeeta Anderson knew that his bum was gone because, as any sensible person knows, a missing bum makes a large dent in the back of a person. You feel like a turtle without a shell,
a donkey
without a tail.

There were other clues, too. When Skeeta sat on the edge of his bed, he slid straight to the floor. Nothing to sit on! Walking from his bedroom to the kitchen he lost his pyjama pants – there was nothing to hold them up!

'Mum!' he called, 'Dad! Something terrible –'

He stopped and stared. His mum and dad were eating breakfast on the floor.

'Morning Skeet,' said his mum.

Skeeta's mouth dropped open like a truck door.

'Ahem,' said Skeeta's dad, sounding very embarrassed. 'We seem to have lost our bottoms in the night. Finding it hard to sit on our chairs. Useful thing, a bottom, when you think of it.'

Skeeta's parents went on eating their toast and drinking their tea.

'Don't be late for school,' said Skeeta's mum.

Skeeta lived in a small town by the sea. The town was called Bugalugs. No one could remember who was to blame for thinking up such a dumb name for a town, and even if they *could* remember, no one was going to own up to it. Because the people of Bugalugs were a bit proud. They were nice folks, but just a teeny bit vain.

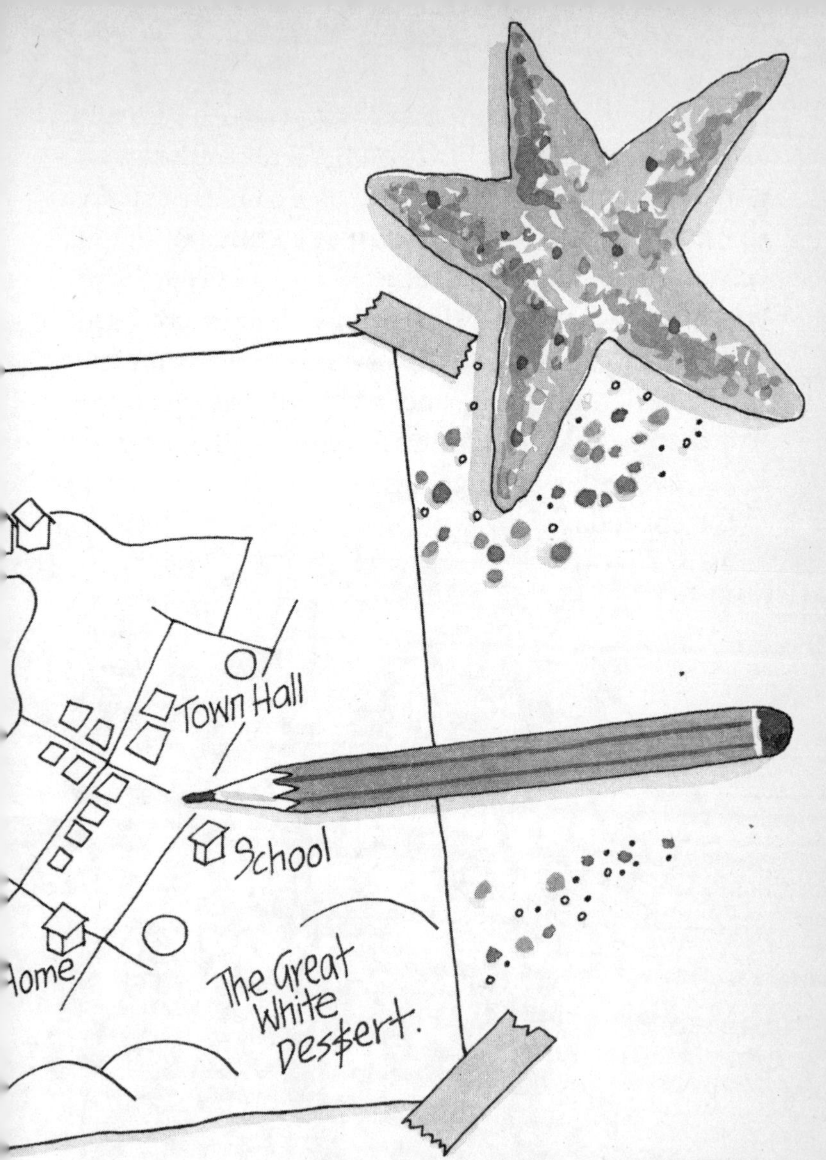

Bugalugs was three streets wide and was built next to a beautiful bay where fishing boats anchored. Behind the town was a great desert of white dunes.

Every morning, before the sun came up over the dunes, the fishermen of Bugalugs went out to catch crayfish. They put fresh bait in their traps every day and the little red critters made gutses of themselves. As all sensible people know, a cray will eat anything except football boots, so bait is not hard to find. Every day crayfish were pulled from the traps, still munching, and were sent all over the world so people could munch on *them*. That's how it was every day at Bugalugs.

Except today.

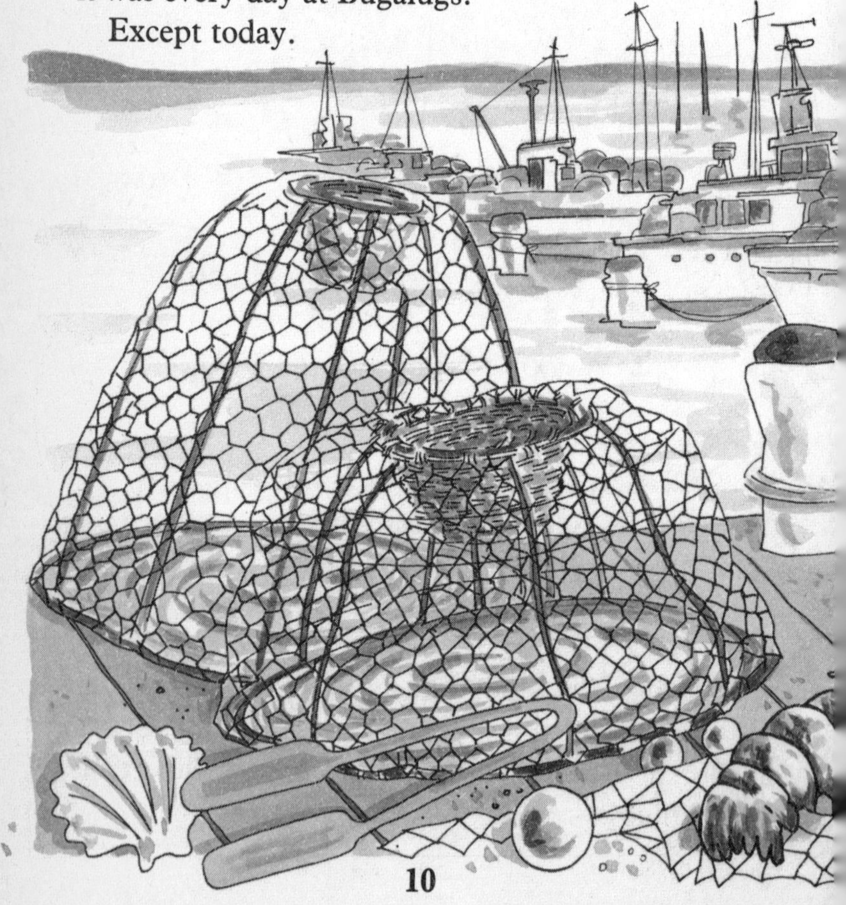

Skeeta went
to the window
and saw
Billy Marbles
trying to ride past
on his bike.
Billy was sliding all
over the place,
with his knees hanging over the
handlebars, and there was Billy's sister Mavis
walking to school with a big
dent in the back of her
dress.

Skeeta ran out into
the street, holding up
his PJ's, and right away
he saw it.
The whole town
was the same.
No bums!

He ran inside and
got dressed quickly.
With some string he
tied his trousers on.

Then he ran to his
best mate's house.

Mick Misery, his best mate, was always getting a hiding. Mick's mum was a real smacker. Smacking was her hobby. She walloped Mick for being early, she whacked him for being late. But this morning she wasn't getting anywhere at all. When Skeeta arrived, Mick's mum was swinging away but every hit just swished past because Mick Misery was *bumless*.

Mrs Misery gave up glumly and sent them off to school. Mick whistled like a drunk canary but Skeeta was worried.

Maybe it's the ozone layer, he thought. Or perhaps we're under attack from aliens. But there had to be an easier answer.

2

It was an awful day at school. With nothing to sit on or hold their pants up with, the kids at Bugalugs Primary didn't get time to learn much. At lunch, Billy Marbles couldn't play doogs at all. As any sensible person knows, a bum gives you balance and you can't be school marble champ without balance. The footy team was useless, the netballers got depressed.

derri
ttom
back
ttock
post
neath
base
seat

During spelling, Mr Wally's shorts suddenly sprang off their safety pins and went scurrying down his long hairy legs like rats out of a tree. The kids laughed. They cacked themselves. *And* they all went home with piles of homework so big they needed their dads' wheelbarrows to get it all home.

After school, instead of doing his homework, Skeeta Anderson decided to do some detective work. He wrote it all out on a piece of paper. No one was talking about it all, embarrassed as they were, but it was pretty clear to Skeeta that:

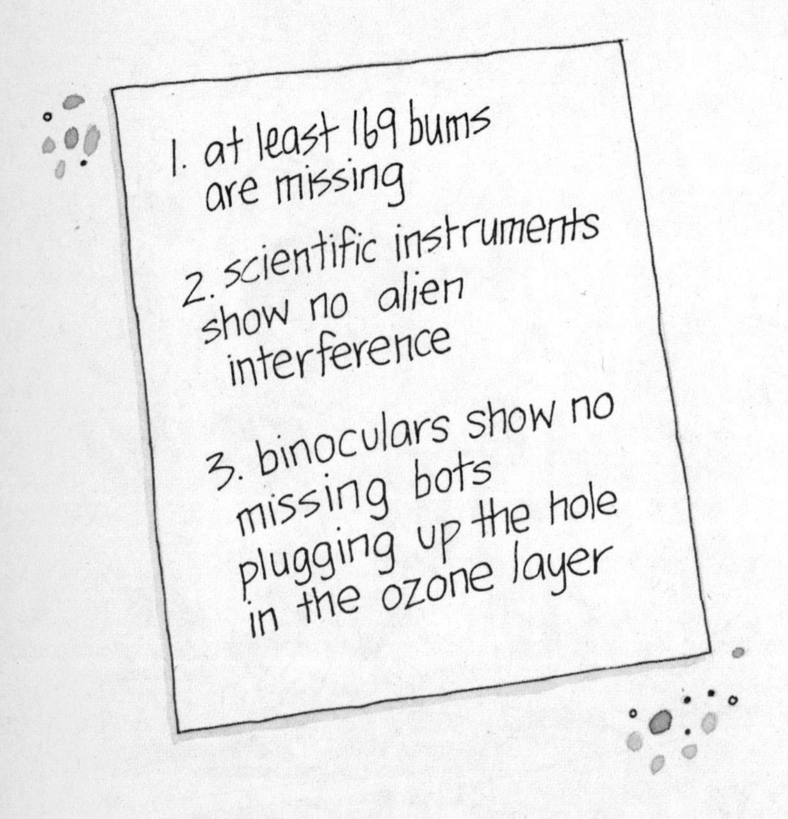

So, he figured: someone must have them. Someone must have burgled them, sneaked into everyone's bedroom with a torch and a pair of salad tongs and got away with the lot!

But Skeeta was a clever kid, a bit of a scientist, really. Because, as any sensible person knows, you can't hide a townful of bums very easily. And in a town where barely anyone has a pair of buttocks to their name, a person getting about still wearing one was definitely SUSPICIOUS.

So Skeeta wired on a pair of running shorts and began to investigate.

At the Bakery, Hairy Hans was sweeping up, looking sad.

'No one wants buns today, Skeet,' said Hans. 'Not that I can blame them. No doughnuts either.'

Nothing suspicious here.

Skeeta went on to Mr Rood the butcher who had a RUMP STEAK SPECIAL sign in his greasy window. That seemed a bit dodgy, today of all days, so Skeeta sneaked a look in the coolroom while the butcher was serving a customer. Nothing. Besides, Mr Rood had been burgled same as everyone else.

Nothing at the general store or the petrol station, and Mrs Huge from the pub looked like a meat pie with a bite taken out of it.

He tried the tip. There was always something useful at the tip, and the price was always right, but no second-hand backsides here today.

In the dunes he saw Mick Misery sliding down slopes having a great time. Skeeta kept out of sight. Mick was the only kid in town enjoying not having something in the back of his shorts and Skeeta didn't want to spoil his fun.

Through the streets of Bugalugs, Skeeta Anderson ran. Dogs snapped at him but missed by a margin. There was nothing suspicious at all, though the number missing must be about four hundred or more by now, he figured.

Down at the beach, windsurfers complained that their wetsuits were turning into sails, and girls in bikinis had to wear suspenders. The seagulls laughed cruelly. Skeeta looked at them hard and long, but they didn't look fat enough to be the culprits. Fishermen stood around looking miserable. They'd all been seasick today and had come in early. As any good fisherman will tell you bums equals balance. But someone on the jetty caught Skeeta's eye.

A fisherman, big and gruff-looking, with tattoos on his arms and a belly under his singlet like a beer barrel, walked right past, and Skeeta's hair stood on end. A-HA! Follow that bum!

Skeeta followed all the way up the beach and down a sand track which led to a big shed with a truck parked out the front. There was the smell of oil and stinky fish and rotten crays, but also a strange pink smell he couldn't quite name.

The man slid the shed door open and went in. All the big, black greasy blowflies that had been sticking to the door suddenly pounced on Skeeta who was trying to hide behind the truck.

Slowly, Skeeta crept forward until he reached the door and put his eye to a crack. What a sight! He turned and ran like fury.

Constable Coma was asleep as usual when Skeeta came busting into the police station, but he woke quickly.

'Strike me pink!' said the constable. 'Someone's stolen me –'

'Everyone's!' said Skeeta. 'Follow me!'

They pounded off to the shed, though not very quickly because Constable Coma kept losing his pants and handcuffs and just about everything else on the way. People noticed them. It wasn't often they saw the policeman running anywhere so they followed. Soon the whole town was on their trail.

It was getting dark when they got to the shed – Skeeta, Constable Coma, and the whole population of Bugalugs. There was a light on inside. Skeeta pulled the door open and everyone roared.

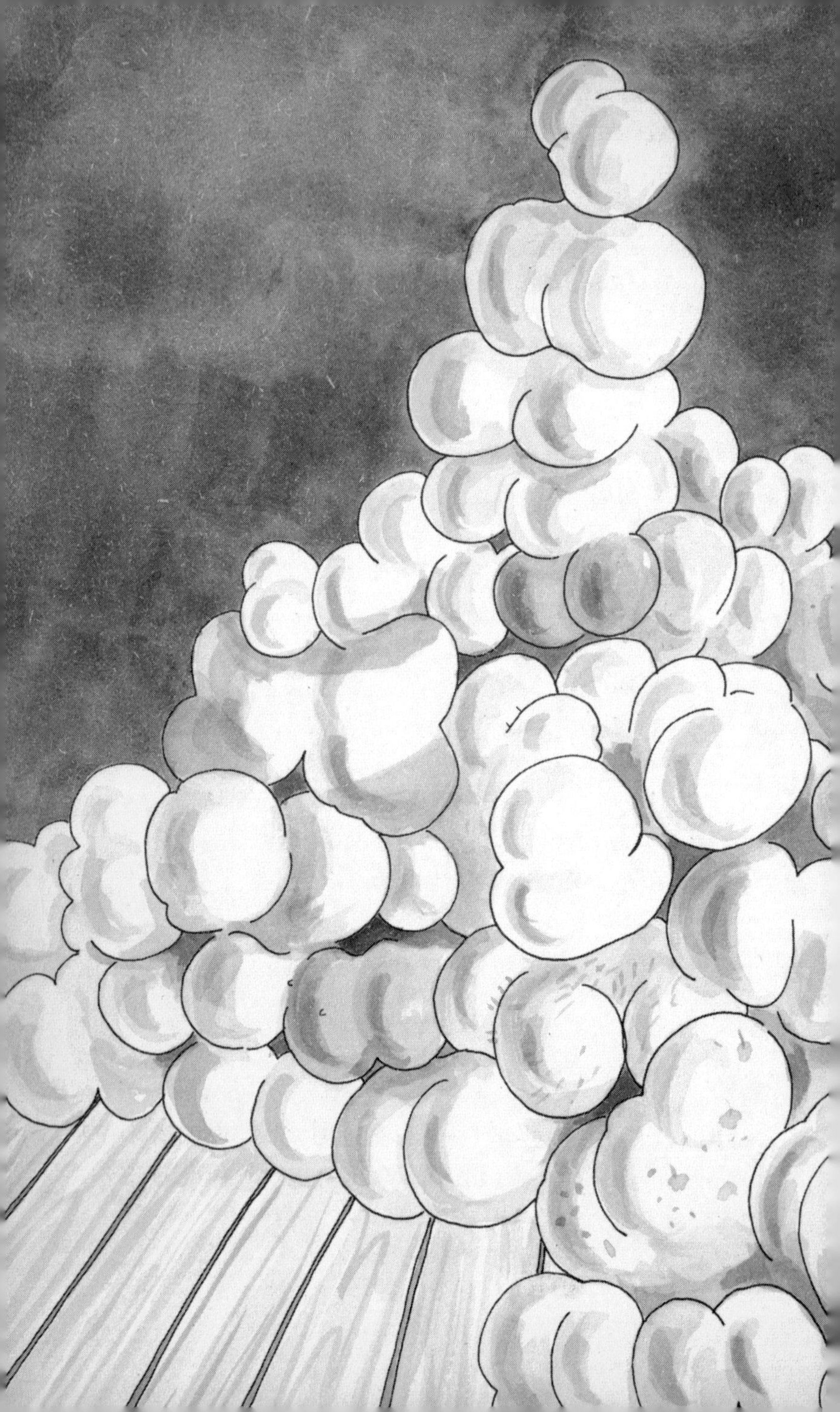

There it was, a gigantic stockpile of human bums, bottoms, backsides and buttocks reaching almost to the roof. Four hundred and ninety-six units, all still in good condition (though some in better shape than others).

'Blue Murphy!'

The fisherman sat down, looking ashamed.

'Why do you need four hundred and ninety-six citizens' bottoms, for goodness sake?' asked Constable Coma.

'For bait,' said Skeeta Anderson.

The crowd growled. Constable Coma put the handcuffs on Blue Murphy and lost his pants yet again.

'Righto, everyone can come inside and claim their own property.'

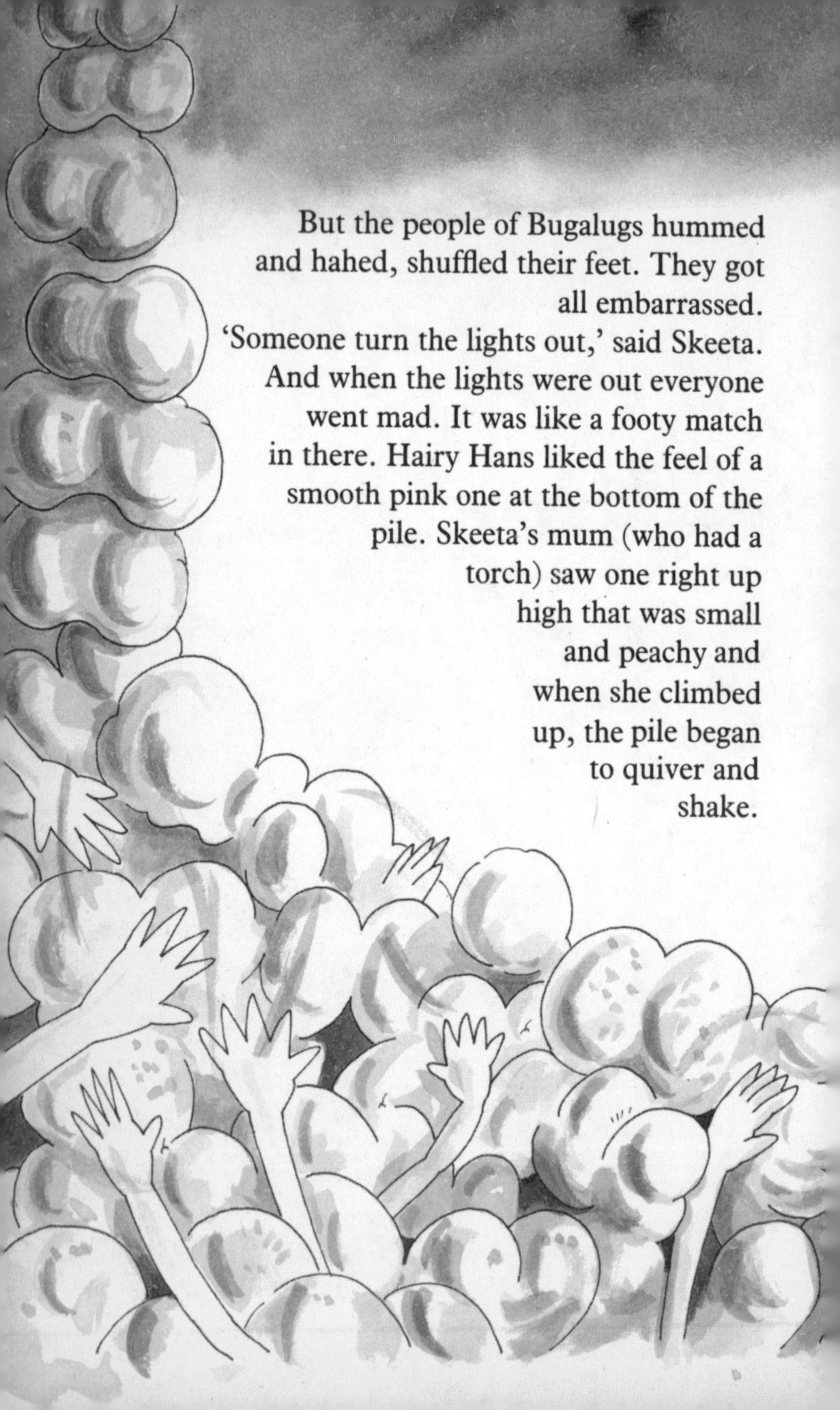

But the people of Bugalugs hummed and hahed, shuffled their feet. They got all embarrassed.

'Someone turn the lights out,' said Skeeta.

And when the lights were out everyone went mad. It was like a footy match in there. Hairy Hans liked the feel of a smooth pink one at the bottom of the pile. Skeeta's mum (who had a torch) saw one right up high that was small and peachy and when she climbed up, the pile began to quiver and shake.

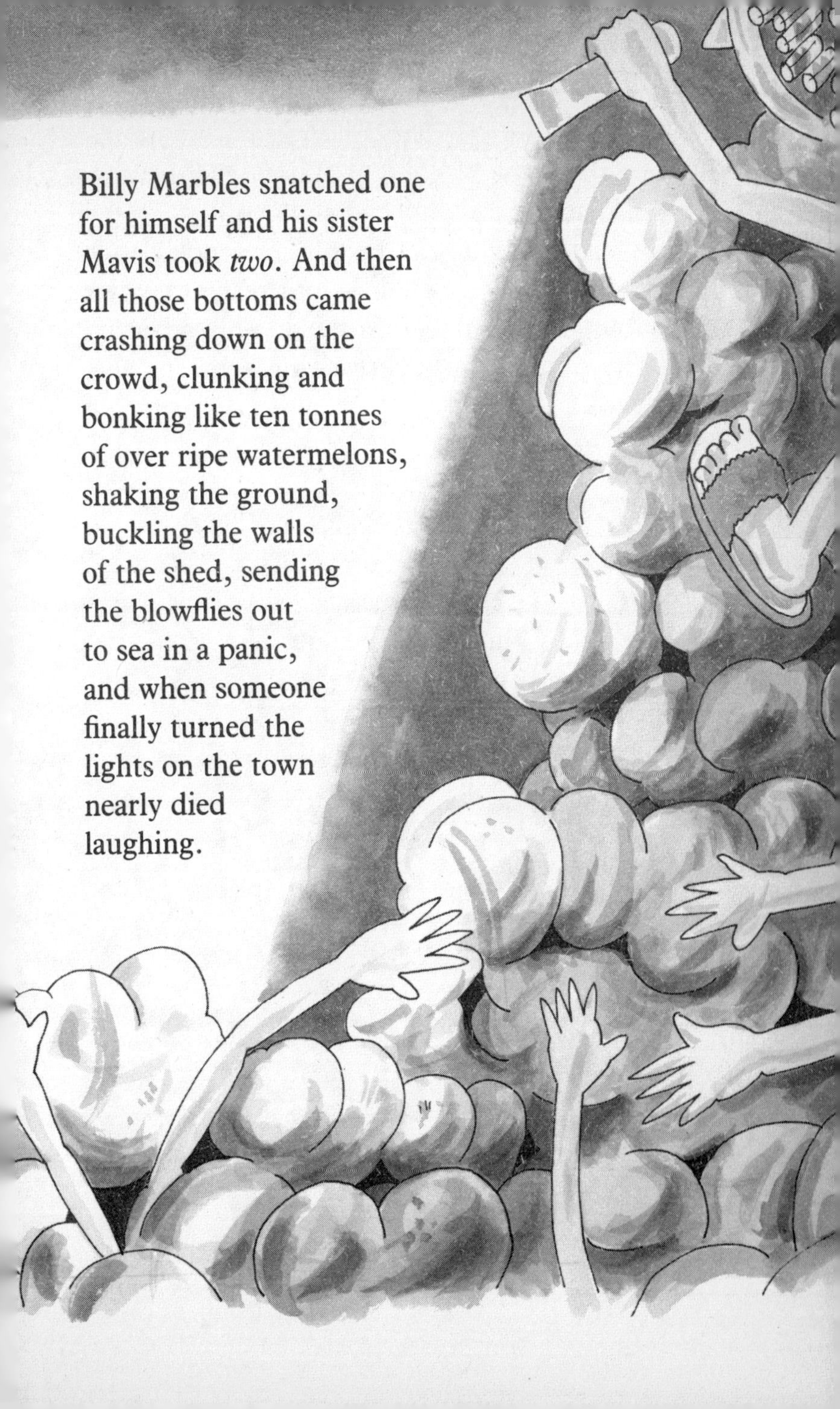

Billy Marbles snatched one for himself and his sister Mavis took *two*. And then all those bottoms came crashing down on the crowd, clunking and bonking like ten tonnes of over ripe watermelons, shaking the ground, buckling the walls of the shed, sending the blowflies out to sea in a panic, and when someone finally turned the lights on the town nearly died laughing.

After that night Bugalugs got back to normal. Well, almost normal. People looked a bit strange. Because they'd all been too proud to take their own bottoms back, fat people had skinny ones and bald people had hairy ones. People pretended to be happy with their new choices, but really they were miserable. It was uncomfortable, unhygenic and altogether unsavoury, like wearing someone else's false teeth.

So next Saturday Skeeta organized a swap-meet in the town hall and everyone got their own back.

All except Skeeta's best mate Mick Misery. Mick did a special deal. He bought Blue Murphy's for twenty-eight cents and three black marbles.

It was too big for him by far, but it was as hard as a brick and his mum gave up smacking him overnight.

Everyone was grateful to Skeeta Anderson. They bought him rump steak, buns and doughnuts and they always thought of him as the kid who caught the Bugalugs Bum Thief.